Emily's
Tears

Ian Minielly

DEDICATION

Dedicated to all the children and families that have lost each other at the hands of government. You are not alone and God is your witness. Justice is coming.

CONTENTS

ACKNOWLEDGMENTS

I would like to acknowledge Jesus as my Lord and Savior. I would also like to thank those who have given me a love of the story and language from my own mom and dad to the assorted teachers and infantryman I have shared a foxhole with or humped a rucksack through the woods next to.

Chapter One: The Invitation

Emily was not expecting a delivery, so when her doorbell rang she checked her phone to see who was standing on her porch. Her porch camera contained the image of an older man, probably in his 60's or 70's with white hair, holding a large mailing packet. He looked harmless enough, probably some kind of door-to-door salesmen or man seeking signatures for some newly sought or opposed legislation she thought. He had that look about him. In other words, he looked normal.

Emily spoke through her phone, which relayed the message to the door speaker, and asked the man to leave the package and she would get it shortly, but she could not come to the door right now. The man looked somewhat startled at the technology speaking to him, even though it had been around for ages, at least in Emily's mind and every other young person born in the 1990s and later.

The old man looked at the door, unaware of where exactly the camera and microphone were located and said, "Ms. Emily, I have instructions from your first mother that I cannot leave here until I have given you this envelope. I am supposed to place it in your own hand and explain some things about it so you will open it right away. I cannot just leave it on your doorstep, I am sorry. I am a man under orders."

Emily was surprised he knew her name, but anyone delivering mail would have the name of the recipient on the package, so he must have read it off the envelope she thought. Then the phrase he used, "First mother," caught her attention. What did he mean by first mother she thought? "Sir, I have only one mother like everyone else, unless you count my biological, but she died in prison. I cannot imagine my mother sending you over here with those instructions. I will call and ask her to confirm."

"Ms. Emily, I am not talking about your birth mother or your aunt Terry. I am talking about your first mother, Ms. Linda Macneely. She is the one who sent me here with the instructions. She is your first mother."

"Sir, I do not know what you mean by first mother, but you are in error. As I said, I have a biological mother who died in prison and I have an aunt who raised me almost from birth. There is no other mother involved, you have the wrong home and person."

"You just said it when you said almost from birth. Ms. Emily, your first mother and father picked you up from the prison after your biological mother gave birth to you. You lived with them for almost two years and they tried to adopt you, but the State decided to give you to your aunt Terry when she threatened to sue them. Ms. Macneely is your first mother and she told me I was not allowed to leave until you had this envelope, so I guess I am camping out on your porch. Thankfully, it is a nice day."

Emily knew there was a transition period between her birth in prison and adoption by her aunt, but she had never been given much information about that time. She always had very vague memories of peace, joy, happiness, and love from those early years, but she did not remember anything concrete and her aunt would never tell her anything about it, beyond saying she was a hostage to some Christians until she was rescued from their home and adopted. Emily had never heard anyone refer to this couple as her first mother and father and it sounded strange. She figured she had better call her aunt, whom she considered her mother, to ask about this.

"Sir, I am going to call my mom and ask her to confirm this before I open the door."

"Ma'am, you can do that if you want and I do not blame you for being careful, us old timers can be pretty scary," he said with a smile, "but I can show you a picture of you and your first mother in the prison the day they picked you up and brought you to their home. I figured you might not welcome me and this picture would possibly do the trick."

Emily watched as Dave Johnson held up a picture to her door, but she could not see the contents of the picture because the camera was in the doorbell. Stifling a laugh, Emily said, "Hold the picture up to the doorbell, that is where the camera is."

Mr. Johnson, chuckling to himself as old people do when caught not quite getting the hang of modern things, held the picture before the doorbell and Emily saw a woman sitting in what looked like a hospital type room holding a small infant with a giant smile on her face. Emily could not see the baby nor could she tell who it was, as her aunt did not have any pictures of her before she was two years old, so she never saw what she looked like as an infant.

"Sir, I do not know who that is or who the baby in the picture is. That could be anyone."

"Ms. Emily, I am a mostly retired private investigator and the Macneelys are my final and last customers. I actually retired years ago, but since this case was on going I never turned it over or dropped it from my workload, as the requirements were minimal. Ma'am, this is going to sound weird, but I have watched you almost your entire life and have been the editor of your life story for the Macneelys since the State gave you to your aunt. I have taken pictures of you at schools, on the playgrounds where you played, and even when you had musicals and recitals. I was there for your first date with George McFarland and when you were a freshman and made the varsity cheer squad, I took your picture for the Macneelys, because they never stopped loving you."

"I know this is a lot to take in, so I want to explain because the more I say it out loud, the weirder it sounds, even to me. Ma'am, the Macneelys love you so much they would not risk

3

confusing you, so they hired me to attend significant life events and capture the events in photos. They hired me to keep them informed of how you were doing. I have been doing this since you were two. I know more about you than almost anyone and if Ms. Macneely wants me to deliver this envelope to you because something big has happened, I am going to do it. This is way outside of our standard protocol. The Macneelys never approached you or wanted me to break their cover and inform you who they were and how much they missed and loved you because it might harm your development."

"Sir, now you are sounding crazy. Are you saying you have been stalking me my whole life?"

"No, ma'am. I never stalked you. The Macneelys wanted to be involved in your life because they love you, but your aunt would not speak to them or share any pictures of your childhood. They could not get any real time information on how you were doing, so they hired me to take snap shots of your life and to keep them informed as best I could from a distance. I know this must sound strange, but it was their love for you and your well-being that kept them away and then Linda, I am sorry, Ms. Macneely, called me three days ago and said her husband Ed had died and he wanted you to know the truth."

"Wait, you mean to tell me my first dad as you call him is dead and now my first mom is reaching out to me for some reason when for 25 years they never once sent a birthday card or Christmas present? These Macneelys sound every bit as weird as my mother said they were when she rescued me from their care."

"Ms. Emily, please let me give you this envelope and take a picture of myself handing it to you. I cannot force you to open it and see what is in there and I cannot force you to read it. My longest clients and some of my most dear friends in life asked me to deliver this to you and this is my final duty in their commission. I can finally retire and sleep knowing a great injustice is being unmasked and you will now know the truth of your past."

"Your first mother and father loved you more than life itself, but they loved you so much they took all the pain of your

4

loss on themselves without burdening you, but now your first daddy has died without being reunited with you. As I said, I cannot make you do anything, but Ms. Macneely asked me deliver this and bring proof you received it and once this is done, ma'am, I will never snap another picture of you again. You will be free of me forever, even though you never knew I was there in the first place."

As the last word left his lips, Emily opened the door with eyes that were watering. The story sounded preposterous, but maybe it was true. She looked at Dave and said, "Come in, let's open this envelope and allow you to get your evidence and leave. I believe you. Let's see what is in there and maybe you can fill in some more blanks for me. This is the craziest thing I have ever heard. They make movies about this kind of plot you know and now you are saying I am smack dab in the middle of it and I never knew? This is settling up to the be weirdest day of my life."

Dave entered Emily's home, handed her the envelope and followed her to the living room. Emily sat down and opened the package and poured the contents onto the coffee table. There was a hand written note in feminine script on top and another card sized envelope addressed to, "My Sweet Baby" in a man's hand writing. In addition to those contents, there were a handful of pictures and a large document that looked like the transcript of a court proceeding.

Dave, seeing the handwritten note said that is Linda Macneely's hand writing as Emily picked up the letter. It read,

> My Dearest Emily,
> I have missed you and loved you your whole
> life. My life has been defined by the pain of
> your loss and the knowledge of the life you
> did not get with us. I have spent a lifetime in
> constant prayer for the life you have grown
> into with your aunt and uncle.
>
> Your father and I have missed you every day
> since they stole you from us and we love you
> dearly. Mr. Johnson is our hero for keeping
> us informed about you and providing us

pictures of as many life events as he could manage. I beg of you to forgive your daddy and I for our failure in not keeping you. We did not understand what we were up against until it was too late and they took you.

We have shed an ocean of tears for you and never stopped loving you. We have faithfully prayed for you, your family, and your future. I wanted to see you so bad, but your daddy was always right when he said we could not confuse you or hurt you, but now he is dead and tasked me to do it.

I regret to inform you your daddy died. I know the one thing he wanted more than anything was to see you, hold you again, read to you as he did when you were ours, and never let go. Unfortunately his life ended before he could ever do any of these things, but I know he would want you at his funeral. We have purposefully delayed the funeral and are keeping Ed on ice to give you time to process all of this and to come see your daddy one last time.

With more love than you could ever imagine,
Linda

Inside the envelope was an invitation to a funeral, scheduled for the next week and an airplane ticket. Fighting through the tears liberally streaming down her face, Emily reached for Dave and hugged him. "Is this all true," she cried into his shoulder?

"Ms. Emily, it is all true, but I am not the person to tell you the whole story. You will have to talk to Ms. Macneely. She would kill me if I told you the whole story. It is not mine to tell. I will say this; I have never known parents that have loved a child as much as they love you. I am a better dad to my own children because of the love they have for you. I have never been this close to pain before and it never went away for them."

"The Macneelys have loved you through the tears and the pain and the misery of knowing you had no idea who they were and how much they missed you and wanted you back. This is all true and your daddy loved you and wanted to see you again, but he died before getting the chance. I have to go now Ms. Emily. My mission is complete and I thank you, but can I take a picture of us to prove I delivered the package and can close this case?"

Emily, almost as if she did not hear Dave, was scanning the pictures he delivered. She saw herself with the cheer squad and her graduations from middle and high school. The day she started her first job after graduating from college and other more innocuous pictures from her past. Emily could see her life captured through the lens of a camera. In one picture she was walking a dog, in another she was playing in the yard with the neighborhood kids, and there were so many more. Her life was captured in a handful of pictures by this man sitting next to her and provided to another family somewhere else who claims they loved her and were her first parents. Emily was thinking this kind of thing does not really happen in real life as tears flowed down her cheeks. Especially to people like her. Emily could not believe how crazy this whole thing was.

Waking up from her thoughts, Emily smiled at Dave and he took their picture. It was one the best ever in his mind, because it captured his subject finally hearing the truth. It was perfect that Emily's tears left truth tracks down her face that were picked up by the camera. Ed Macneely would be able to rest now that his sweet baby knew who he was. It was just so unfortunate he died before he could have peace with this girl he always called his daughter.   Dave prepared to leave, hugged Emily again, only this time without asking and unprompted, as he knew it would be their last time together and handed her his business card. He said he was officially retired now, but he would always be available for her if she ever needed anything and he loved her too. This private investigator that had spent more than two decades following her and detailing her life for the parents she never knew, admitted he loved her like she was his own lost child.

As the door closed behind him, tears for this broken family began streaming down Dave's own face. These were Emily's tears in Dave's mind. He was shedding them for her and the lost decades of love she never knew existed and the two people who hurt for her every single day because the State destroyed this family. Emily had changed the whole course of his life and she had no idea.

When the Macneelys contacted him twenty-five years ago, he was an alcoholic in the process of ruining his marriage and destroying his own family. Their story of pain and suffering and how well they bore it woke him up to his own life and his wife and kids. Emily and the Macneelys saved his marriage, his family, and his kids, and none of them knew it.

Dave never told the Macneelys how close he was to losing everything when they contacted him with a weird job request. As the tears streamed down his cheeks Dave thought about how he never informed them as he took these pictures and relayed the information back to the Macneelys while cashing their checks, how his life was being healed through their grace and suffering. Dave could not stand the thought of their pain and the missed love they all experienced whether they knew it or not, so he began pouring more of himself into his own family and quit drinking.

Dave was the man he was today, a respected elder in his Baptist church, because of Emily and her loss. How could he ever relay that to someone without hurting them or sounding corny? So he stayed silent and thanked God for the Macneelys and Emily's tears, because they saved his life. People have no idea what seeds they plant through their actions and love or what seeds they water. Dave's testimony involved a broken family unknowingly healing his own and his church knew it well and always remembered Emily in their prayers.

Dave did not get far after pulling away from Emily's. He only drove about two blocks before pulling over, blinded by love, tears, and compassion to the point he could not see well enough to drive. It had taken more than two decades to get to this point, but Dave was finally going to close this chapter. It was his last case and his most important. This case defined his life and it was thankfully over.

Dave knew he could not call Ms. Macneely to confirm delivery of this special package because he could not get the words out. He and Linda Macneely had talked so many times over the years and he had heard her cry a thousand times, but he knew he would not be able to keep it together on his end this time. Dave looked at the picture he just took of Emily sitting on her couch, holding the envelope and all the other pictures and things from Linda, and fresh Emily tears flowed down his face again.

Dave set down his phone. He grabbed the box next to him in the seat and began looking at the contents. Inside were pictures of Emily from his first assignment through today, after he added this newest picture. Three lives and lost love were contained in the box. He knew while the chapter was closing for him and had ended for Ed with his death, Emily and Linda were just opening a new chapter and who knew where it would go.

Would Emily accept Linda? Would Linda be able to hold it together without Ed? Linda did not agree with staying away from Emily and silent. She had always wanted to barge in on Emily's life. The physical and emotional distance from Emily had been worse for her than anyone. Dave wondered how well she would handle all of this alone, but looking at the picture on his phone again, Dave realized she might not be alone after all.

Chapter Two: Truth Revealed

Emily closed the door behind Dave and slid to the floor, coming to rest on her behind and heels. What just happened, she asked herself? She had been having a normal day before the doorbell rang. Now she has a family that she never knew and she learned they consider her their daughter? But what about my aunt and uncle, they have raised me and been there my whole life? Aren't they my family and how in the world did all of this happen and who in the world is Dave and why has he been taking pictures of me my whole life?

There was just too much information to process in one sitting. Emily knew she had always felt sadness. She had never known her biological mother and father and it was always painful to think about. Her mother died in prison and her biological dad was still there and would never be released. He had written a handful of times over the years, but mostly was just trying to get by in prison and never seemed to care much. Her aunt and uncle had always been there and they always said they rescued her. Whether they knew it or not they always made her feel guilty because she came along unexpected in their life.

Her aunt and uncle had done a great job providing for her. Emily had no complaints. She never wanted for anything and always had more than enough to eat and wear. When she went to college, they paid the bill and kept her debt free so she could start life in the catbird seat. Her aunt and uncle were great and she loved them, but she never felt loved by them.

While they always said they rescued her, now that she met Dave and saw these pictures and read the letter from Linda, what exactly did they rescue me from she could not help but think? The Macneelys sure seemed loving and they obviously never gave up on me, even though they could not be there for me. Could the Macneelys be the answer to the void in my life that had led me to tears so many times?

While thinking about all these things, Emily noticed the unopened card in the pile of memories she poured out. How could she have let Dave leave without knowing its contents, she thought? Maybe some additional insight would be in the card that would help make sense of it all. Maybe she could get a better feel for the Macneelys and what happened since she obviously had no idea and it was all news to her.

Emily always thought she was adopted by her aunt and uncle after a short period in foster care, she had no idea she had spent so long with foster parents. She had no idea they had wanted to adopt her and had actually fought to keep her. How could no one have told her about all of this? Emily thought no one had ever fought for her, but now she was learning that was not true. With her ears ringing from the blood pressure, Emily pulled herself off the floor, wiped the tears off her face, and grabbed the unopened envelope.

The envelope was yellow. In the obvious handwriting of a man, Emily read, "My Sweet Baby" on its face again and ran her fingers over the words. Emily spent a few moments imagining a man holding the envelope and writing those words to her and only to her. To Emily's scrutiny, it looked like old tear stains marred the outside of the envelope. She could detect faint water splotches that had been quickly wiped away. Was Ed Macneely crying when he wrote, "My Sweet Baby," on the envelope and sealed it?

Carefully opening the envelope, Emily pulled out a card with a Maine Coon cat wearing a Seahawks jersey on the front. Emily had always loved the Seahawks, so it was eerie seeing this beautiful cat wearing her favorite football teams jersey. The card said, "Meow loves you more than catnip." Written on the opposite side was a heart drawn by hand with her name and "forever" written inside of the heart. The card was kind of goofy and childish, like a man would buy, but it also contained a hand-written note.

Dear Emily,

I am sure you do not remember, but I am your daddy. When I came home from work, you would run to the door saying, "Daddy, daddy, daddy," and grab a book for me to read to you. This was our routine every day. You were my girl and I was your daddy. I read to you every single day and we always talked about your future. I never knew until you were gone, we would not have that future together.

I want you to know your mother and I never stopped loving you. The State may have kidnapped you from us, but we never gave up on you. We have prayed for you every single day, as have thousands of other people in the Southern Baptist Convention. I have mentioned you in hundreds of sermons and writings and you were always on my mind. I always filled out prayer cards for you that tens of thousands of people would pray over every year.

I am sorry I was not able to protect you and keep you. I failed you and I am sorry. I was naive. I thought God would protect you and we had no risk of losing you, but I was wrong. I have never been able to adequately explain why God allowed you to be taken. Neither your mom nor I have been able to figure it out or understand. I beg of you to not hold this against your mother or God.

Linda always wanted to break into your life. I convinced her it would do more harm than good and risk causing you issues. I convinced your momma the best thing we could do was stay away and love you silently and pour our hearts out to God with prayer on your behalf. We have done this and God is good. We have watched you flourish and achieve success and grow into the most beautiful woman in the world and we have loved you every single day since we brought you home from prison.

Please do not hold anything against your aunt and uncle. We think they were told lies about us as people and as parents and they think they did a good thing adopting their niece. Please do not hold this against them. We gave them and you the space needed to allow you to grow, but we have loved you from afar every single day.

There is not a single facet of your mother's life or mine that are not tempered by our loss of you. Everyday you were with us, even if you were not physically here. Please do not forget that we loved you first and always and had no choice when we lost you. The State and its corrupt minions took you for a ransom and gave you away, wrecking our loving family.

While I must be dead and gone if you are reading this, I will wait for you patiently at the gates to heaven because I have not felt you hug me in decades and I miss it. I was your daddy then and I am still your daddy now. I want to wait a long time to hug you again though, so do nothing to hurry the date up.

I have the best companion a man could have in Jesus. He assures me you are in good

hands and He has watched over you closely
since birth, hearing all of our prayers and
answering all the best ones and that it was
Him who brought us together all those years
ago, for moments just like this.
Love your daddy, and please be patient with
your mom, she is a handful and has missed
you so bad for so many years that it almost
killed her many times,
Your Pop
PS We never stopped loving you and even if
we only had two years together, they were the
best two years of our lives. We love you!

It took Emily an hour to finish the short letter. Bouts of
tears closed her eyes and made it impossible for her to read
another word. Then she would blow her nose, wait for her eyes
to clear and read another sentence before the pain and love of
the letter overwhelmed her again. By the time she finished the
letter, she wanted to read it again in one sitting, but she
couldn't. Over and over she started reading the letter, trying to
get through it in one sitting, but she could not. The love and
passion from Ed Macneely was too clear. Emily was loved
deeply and she never even knew it. Who were these people?

Emily knew she needed to talk to her mom. She needed to
hear what happened from her mom's lips as she processed the
fact another family had wanted her and lost to her aunt and
uncle. Who were these people that picked her aunt and uncle
over the Macneelys and why did these other people want to
adopt her and why were they denied? This was all just too
much to handle. Emily had to talk to her mom. Are these
people even sane or is someone just pulling her leg? Is this all
true or are they just crazy she could not help thinking.

Pulling into her parents' driveway, Emily started crying
again. She decided she needed to sit and compose herself before
seeing her aunt and uncle. How would they react to this news?
How would they respond knowing Ed and Linda Macneely had
reached out to her and had spent years having her followed?

Emily's aunt and uncle had taken her in and adopted her
from her deadbeat parents she always thought, and now she

was showing up to question them about her beginning moments and time? Emily realized as she sat in the car waiting to go in, this is why I never saw pictures of myself as an infant. All of the family pictures started when she was around two, she always just figured she must have been an ugly baby or they were not proud of her for some reason. Now she realized her earliest years were with the Macneelys.

Her phone buzzed and it was her mom. Her mom had noticed her sitting in the car and texted her. "You coming in? What's going on? Are you pregnant?" Emily silenced her phone and looked in the rear view mirror. Her eyes were blood red and her cheeks covered in tears. She looked rough, but there was not much she could do now, so she headed in. Knocking on the door her mom answered, "Why are you knocking goofy…" but then Terry noticed how rough Emily looked.

"What is going on dear? What happened? Did someone hurt you? Have you been raped?"

"I don't know," Emily said through her tears.

"What do you mean you don't know? If you were raped you would know!" Terry wrapped her arms around Emily and ushered her towards the living room. They sat down together and Emily cried into her aunt's shoulder, staining the shirt with her tears and mascara. After a few minutes of tears, Emily was able to stifle their flow as her mom rubbed her shoulders.

"Mom, I received an invitation to Ed Macneely's funeral today. What do you know about him?"

"Who?"

"Ed Macneely, my first dad."

"Emily, your first dad is in prison and your second dad is at work. The Macneelys were never your parents. They were just foster parents and they were nasty people and we rescued you from them and saved you from their Christian lifestyle and cult. The Macneelys are bad people and I am glad Ed is dead. I have silently cursed them more times than I care to remember. They fought us like cats and dogs and cost us thousands of dollars in lawyer fees to win you. You are lucky to live here with us and not those whackos."

"Mom, the Macneelys do not sound bad. They sound like people who wanted to adopt me. I have letters from them and they appear very loving and normal. They even said they purposefully stayed away after I was taken so as not to cause any problems for you and dad raising me, even though it hurt them badly. Crazy people don't do that."

"Emily, the Macneelys are bad. You have no idea how bad of parents they were. They were starving you and kept you caged. We heard all about it from the adoption worker. Those people were Christian radicals who would have brainwashed you into their cult. Do you know they are Southern Baptists? We saved you from their hell by threatening DHHS that we would sue if we did not get custody of you. You have no idea how terrible those Macneelys are. We heard so many stories from the adoption worker about them. It would make your head spin! Those people actually believe the Bible is true and try to live by its standards!"

"Mom, how do you know all those things you heard are true? Whatever you heard about them? How do you know they are true?"

"Emily, why would the adoption worker and the guardian ad litem lie about it? They both said you were being retarded in their care and it was necessary for us to get you as soon as possible to keep you from being damaged permanently. If they shaved some corners to make it happen, it was all for the better. And now look at you, a successful career, a college graduate, and levels of achievement many would beg for at your young age. We did this for you. Who knows what kind of freak you would have turned into if they had been allowed to raise you. You should thank your dad and I for adopting you and saving you from that Christian lifestyle and all their voodoo and hocus pocus."

"Mom, I am very thankful you adopted me, don't get me wrong, but what if there is more to the story than you heard? You just said you threatened DHHS for custody, which is something the Macneelys also said. What if they were not so bad and the stories you heard were not true? What if the stories were just stories and fabricated?"

"Emily, I do not even know why it matters. Your dad and I raised you and made you into the person you are today. You just said Ed is dead, so who cares anyways? You should not worry yourself about them whackos. I would stay away if I were you and just ignore their ranting. Those people are fundamentalists and crazy. I would not doubt them even being Republicans!"

"Oh mom…. Why didn't you pick me up from the prison? Why did they pick me up from prison and not you if they were so bad? If they were so bad, why did they stay away the last twenty-five years and allow you and dad to raise me without any problems or interference from them? Why did they send a picture of me in Linda Macneely's arms in the prison on the day they picked me up? Why were you and dad not there? Why did they pick me up instead of you?"

"Baby, I have had enough of this. We have not talked about the Macneelys in this house for over twenty years because we hate them. They tried to keep you and you are my loser brother's daughter! They wanted to raise you to know the Lord, they said. You would not imagine how rude they were. Did you know that Linda Macneely contacted me once before we took you? She said they loved you and wanted to adopt you. I turned her in as crazy to the adoption people!"

She said to me, "Mother to mother, I should back off and allow them to adopt you because they loved you and had you from birth. That as a mother I should know how much love they have for you. Those people are crazy and we saved you from them Emily. I will not have this conversation with you again. You are not going to Ed's funeral Emily. If you do, you will go over my dead body."

After Emily stopped crying at the harsh words of her aunt, she got up. She could not believe the way her mom had spoken to her about her past and the Macneelys. Looking at her mom, she could not believe the difference in tone coming from her. She had only heard her mother speak this way about Christians and Republicans over the years. Her mother was being harsh towards the Macneelys when they had stayed away to keep me from suffering, she thought. Seeing how her mom reacted, Emily figured the Macneelys were right to stay away. It does appear as if there is no way they could have all gotten along well enough for me to have a relationship with them. Emily stood up and walked towards the door before her mom began addressing her again.

"Emily, please stay way from the Macneelys. It has been twenty-five years since you came to live with us. Do you really think they have your interests in mind if they stayed away over 20 years? Obviously they have something in mind and I do not want you to get hurt. You cannot trust Christians Emily. Stay away from them, I am warning you."

"OK mom, I have a lot to think about. I will call you later, thanks," and Emily opened the door and left her adoptive mother standing silently and cursing the Macneelys for having reached out.

Chapter Three: What To Do?

As Emily drove home, she could not believe how her mom reacted. The Macneelys had left them alone for over 20 years. The Macneelys had obviously loved her very much, although it was pretty strange to find out they had hired a private investigator to follow her and take pictures regularly. This was either the actions of crazy people or the actions of people who loved her and never wanted to lose her, but loved her enough they did to want to cause any problems. The Macneelys seemed to have been very calculated on her behalf, but had also suffered greatly for their generosity.

Emily, with tears streaming down her face, pulled the car over to the side of the road and just cried tears of sadness over what she did not know and the past she never had. She simply could not see the road well enough through her tears to drive safely. With her head buried in her hands, Emily cried like she had never cried before. As she sat crying, she heard her uncle's snide comments in the back of her mind every time she had cried as a kid, "Here come more Emily tears, lets all watch out and make sure she gets her way again." What kind of life did she miss out on she could not help but ask herself?

Emily loved her uncle, but he never seemed to love her back. He provided well enough and took care of her throughout her life, but he had never once told her he loved her. She always craved a father's love growing up and she now realized there was a time she had it. All these years she thought it was her uncle who held her, read to her, and loved on her when she was a toddler, but now she realized it was Ed Macneely! Ed Macneely had been the father she always wanted but was not allowed to have, and the tears flowed even faster.

It was amazing now that she realized the sentiment and feelings were misplaced on her uncle and that he had never been the dad she wanted or needed. He had been a checkbook and security officer keeping her safe and sound, but he had never been her daddy. Her daddy was out East and loved her so much he stayed away so she would not be confused. Emily could not believe the dad she always wanted was present in the background, but was taken from her by the State. How much had she missed because of corrupt bureaucrats?

It was impossible to consider what her life would have been like had she stayed with the Macneelys. The only thing she could clearly say is she would have never missed the father she did not have, because now that she had seen a picture of Ed, the face jived perfectly with her memories and the images in her mind she thought were her uncle. She remembered Ed much more clearly, but only in a series of fleeting memories from her earliest years. Emily decided she was going to need to scour her mind and see what other memories she might have of the Macneelys and how she had confused them with her aunt and uncle all these years. What did I miss out on she asked herself?

Emily looked in her rear view mirror and saw the black mascara streaking down her face. Could she go to the funeral for a man she barely remembered, but who clearly loved her? What kind of pressure would be on her if she showed up? Would her one-time foster mom try and move in and become active in her life and put pressure on her? Emily did not know if she could handle something like that. This was all so strange and awkward. Emily did not want to go to a funeral, but she even more did not want to go to a funeral where she was the person on display instead of the dead body.

What would Linda Macneely say to her? Emily had these memories flooding back into her mind of her earliest days. Memories that had long been suppressed or forgotten were coming back. She remembered spending time with Linda, resting on her chest and taking naps as they watched Christmas specials and old television shows. Thinking of this, Emily realized now why she liked I Love Lucy, The Cosby Show, and Daniel Tiger's Neighborhood. I watched these shows with Linda Macneely!

Emily began deeply mourning Linda as she realized just how great of an impact Linda and Ed had on her life before she was taken from them. In less than two years the Macneelys had a timeless impact on her loves, likes, and even dislikes and she never knew why. How could the Macneelys have given her up? How could they let her aunt take her from them when they seemed to love her so much? Could she really go to the funeral of a man who had allowed her to be taken? What kind of love would allow that?

When Emily got home, she sent her best friend a text, "I need to talk. Are you available? Come over as soon as you can. You will not believe what happened today."

Emily's friend Sammy texted back within five minutes, "The Salon closes in three hours, but I can leave anytime as I do not have any more appointments today. Do you need me now or can you wait a couple of hours?"

"Can you come now?"

"Sure, I will be there soon. Put the tea on, or if it is really heavy, put on some of that good coffee you like to drink."

Emily decided the news she was going to break to Sammy would require afternoon coffee. She always preferred to start her day with green tea and then 1-2 cups of medium roast coffee to close out the morning, but this kind of information would require afternoon coffee, which was a real rarity for her.

The door rang and Sammy swept into the apartment with her typical flourish. Leave it to a professional hair stylist to be full of drama when someone else had more drama then they could handle in their life. Sammy poured a cup, said she would drink it black because she liked the flavor anyways, and asked Emily what was going on? Sammy said she could not remember anytime in their friendship Emily had drama in her life so when she texted and said she needed to talk, Sammy knew it was big.

"Alright Em, what is going on? You are like the least drama queen I know, which is not really saying much when you consider all the queens I know in the hair business."

"Sammy, look at this," as Emily handed Sammy the whole package she had received from Dave Johnson, the private investigator. "A PI came by today and gave me this package and said my first mother and father wanted me to come to the funeral of my first father next week."

"What do you mean first mother and father? I thought I saw your dad last week and he looked healthy enough."

"No Sammy, not my uncle Bill. My first dad, Ed Macneely, is being buried next week."

"What do you mean your first dad? I know Bill is your uncle and Terry is your aunt, but I thought your mom and dad were in prison or died already?"

"Yes, my biological mother died and my biological father is still in prison, but I lived with Ed and Linda Macneely before my aunt and uncle. They were my foster parents out east before my aunt and uncle adopted me for two years."

"Well can you really call them your first mom and dad? They sound like foster parents, not a mom and dad."

"They were foster parents, but according to the investigator they tried to adopt me and even fought the State when they decided to give me to my aunt and uncle. The PI said my first mom and dad loved me deeply and were permanently hurt by losing me and had hired him to follow me and take my picture periodically to keep them informed."

"Wow, that kind of sounds creepy. They hired some guy to follow you? And to take your picture? How long has this been going on?"

"Look at the pictures. There are pictures in there of me from grade school through graduation from high school and college. They apparently wanted to keep details of me for their records or something, I really do not know. Why would they want pictures but never contact me? Doesn't that sound weird to you?"

"Well what reason did they give or did you get one at all?"

"The PI said they did not want to confuse me. He said they wanted the pictures and information about me so they could still feel involved, but they did not want to risk hurting me or causing me any kind of issues. The investigator seemed relieved to speak with me, although he seemed sad because it was him talking to me and not my first mom and dad as he kept referring to them. He seemed to think they were really good people who had suffered a catastrophic loss and just could not accept I had been taken from them, but who also could not bring themselves to hurt me by trying to force themselves into my life."

"Well what does your mom say? Has your dad said anything about it? What are they saying about the Macneelys?"

"My aunt, I just do not think I can ever call her my mom again, says the Macneelys are terrible because they are Christians. She said I was lucky to have been rescued from their care by her and my uncle."

"So your aunt is not a fan of the Macneelys. Well can you blame her? It sounds like they are Christians and you know how much she hates Christians. Are you surprised she feels like she rescued you from them? I have never met someone more hostile to a group of people when she does not even know any that I am aware of. It makes you wonder what God ever did to her for her to hate Christians as badly as she does."

"You know how liberal she is Sammy. She loves all things progressive and since Christians are opposed to many of the things she loves, she hates them. But do you think I should go? Should I travel out east next week for the funeral? They included a round trip ticket for me and it is even in the first class seating section and from the sounds of it, they are not rich people."

"I do not know Em. It is really weird and you do not know if they are crazy or not. They always stayed in the background and apparently just wanted to know how you were doing? That does kind of sound like something people would do who loved someone. It does sound like they loved you and want you to come out there for the funeral. What harm could it do? It is not like they ever had reason to keep doing this other than they loved you. I mean they did include a First Class ticket!"

"Honestly Em, if my parents loved me as much as it sounds like these Macneelys loved you, I think my whole life would be different. I kind of want you to go out there so you can come back here and tell me about it. This is some real Hollywood drama and you are right smack dab in the middle of it. I am jealous of you. You not only had this rich upbringing by your snotty aunt and uncle, you had these poor people who loved you more than life itself and suffered in silence for twenty some odd years to keep you from suffering. That is some real crazy love and I would like to hear more about it."

Chapter Four: The Truth Unmasked

When the image of Emily and Dave came across Linda Macneely's phone, she nearly dropped her coffee cup and she was a well-known coffee snob. Linda loved to drink the finest of coffees, but then she added a bunch of half and half and sugar and masked the taste of the quality. Ed always said he could buy cheap coffee and she would never even know as much junk as she doctored it with.

Seeing the image of Emily and Dave was the confirmation she needed that Emily knew of their existence and that the formal invitation to Ed's funeral was in her grasp. After so many years and so many tears shed without Emily, Linda finally shed some tears knowing Emily knew the truth about her beginning. Emily was learning her genesis account, thought Linda. Emily had this great beginning that she was totally unaware of and Linda and Ed had suffered in silence for decades, but no more. Now she was going to hear and learn and find out why her aunt and uncle adopted her and how they had lost her. It was the moment Ed and Linda had been waiting to experience; only Ed did not live long enough to see it.

No one knew what it was like to lose a child, unless they had lost a child themselves. Linda thought of all the people who tried to offer condolences over the years. People with good intentions saying the aunt and uncle sounded like they would provide a good upbringing. These people all meant well, but the words were like daggers to the people who had lost their child. Whether they lost their child because the State stole them or through an accidental or untimely death. The pain was unbearable and never went away.

Good-natured people would say God was involved in the process and would look out for Emily or that Emily was blessed to have even more people that loved her. All of it was painful and all of it hurt. Every single time some well-meaning family member or friend said something like that, it cut right through their soul and would result in another sleepless night of misery and pain over their daughter that was stolen. Unless that kind of loss is felt first hand, a person just cannot understand the depth of the hurt, but for those that knew, they recognized it in other people. They were a silent class of sufferers.

Sure, the aunt and uncle would provide a roof, food, and education, but did they provide the same kind of love as the Macneelys? This question would just burn the Macneelys up because they would never know. Something so simple, was Emily being loved? If she was, then where were they when she was born in a prison hospital? Did they drive through the snowstorm to rescue her? They knew all about her before she born. The biological mother and father had kept them apprised the whole time, but they never came forward or put in a claim to adopt her then. It was almost as if they waited to see she was healthy and thriving before they made their move and threatened the State for possession.

Did they spend the first six-months watching her uncontrolled tremors as her little body expunged the poisons she was bathed in inside the womb? No one but Ed knew how Linda spent months of sleepless nights comforting Emily and soothing her cries as the bond between them deepened and the poisons were filtered out. No one else was there those nights worrying and praying over her little body and asking God to heal her and make her well. Only Ed and Linda knew this feeling and how close they had grown towards Emily.

Losing Emily was crushing and the people at DHHS and the adoption agency were completely callous about it. They would regularly call Linda and Ed, "nothing more than foster parents," as if they were only watching her for the small allowance provided by the State. The cases and individuals involved meant nothing to the State workers. Their goal was to maximize their profit from each case, which often meant getting cases decided within the time frame allowed by the federal government for large bonuses to get paid out.

Those elements of State power were not there, as Linda suffered not only the loss of her daughter, but also the uncertainty of her future in the hands of others. They were the causative agent of the problem, not any kind of solution. All the decisions a mom and dad make regarding their children, would now be made by someone else in Emily's case. These decision makers had a different set of criteria and would almost certainly make different choices. Their choices were based on finances and politics. Over the years Ed and Linda learned about many different cases within DHHS and how the same people would game plan the adoptions and decisions to spread the wealth and keep everyone happy. It was always the same group of people profiting and it was not the families or the children.

Knowing the people involved in Emily's case were making decisions on how best it impacted their bottom line was nothing short of dishonest. This very thought burned the Macneelys every night and it never went away. The most wicked people imaginable would pursue jobs in the social services profession and would be trained in how to seize children and destroy lives, while increasing their own bottom lines to the point they would even get bonuses. The whole process is sickening to people on the outside, but the State will not reform it.

Ed and Linda talked about Emily every single day from the moment she was stolen until Ed died. The loss of Emily was profound and forever changed all three of their lives. It was poor decision and God had placed many people in positions to make the correct choice, but each one of them went with the State and chose not to pursue justice, but their own selfish ends. Emily's case was a travesty of justice and cases like hers happened everyday.

The Macneelys prayed for Emily constantly because she experienced so many traumas in her early years from the womb until the day she was stolen and inserted into a foreign and strange family. Her biological mother and father were drug-fueled train wrecks who had no moral business fornicating and having children. They had rap sheets a mile long with drug charges and felony bank robbing convictions across many states and nothing stopped them from repeating the same sins over and over again, until each arrest. Between the two of them they had 15 children before Emily, thankfully she was their last. Emily was conceived under the worst of circumstance without any choice in the matter, but her future was bright as Linda reflected on how much she grew in their two years together.

Most kids learn the word, "no" early and say it all the time and it tends to infuriate parents. Emily loved to say, "yes." She would walk around the Macneely home, grabbing things and look at Linda or Ed saying, "yes?" and they would say, "yes," and explain what it was. Emily would grab a book and bring it to Ed and say, "yes?" and Ed would say, "Yes, my sweet baby, lets read together," or something similar. All day and night Emily would grab something and look at Ed and Linda and say, "yes." Not only was it the cutest thing in the world to witness first hand, but also it showed Emily's sweetness from an early age and how bright her future would be. She was not your normal kid; Emily was exceptional.

Linda planned to introduce piano; Ed wanted her to play guitar and banjo. Both of them agreed she had a great future singing in church and leading people to Christ through her personal story and journey. Emily's future was bright and they knew it.

It always bothered them when a lawyer they hired initially said they should let her go when they brought their case to him. He said they would be better off without her as much as it hurt today. Kids like her seemed sweet he said, but in his experience they would turn out bad. By the time they reached puberty he explained, the children of drug addicts become handfuls in school and begin acting out. By the time they turn twenty he claimed, drug baby's would have a record and begin their long descent towards a life in and out of prison.

The lawyer explained this is not certain of course, but in his long-tenured experience in working with foster and adoptive parents through the State's court system, his experience showed heartache was almost always the end result. The parents would spend thousands to get custody and pour themselves into these children, but the end result was the drugs in the womb and the poor conditions of the mothers in almost every instance could not be overcome, no matter how much love was poured into them. The Macneelys explained they understood, but Emily was different and she was special.

The lawyer, Linda recalled, said every single Christian foster parent said the same thing to him and he would take their money, but he always urged them to release the kids and be free of the future burden. "The system" would label them abusive and bad parents once the kids began acting out. When the trouble would come, the kids and the foster system and the biological parents would be given a free pass for all the damage that was done and all the blame and all the trauma would be heaped on the Christian family that tried to do the right thing.

He said he saw it every week in his profession because the system was so broken and they should just let Emily go. He said they would be better off in the long run because if they didn't, in fifteen years they would be contacting him again about legal needs for some trouble Emily got in. Linda remembered Ed telling this attorney that his experience was not indicative of every child and Emily was different. They had her from birth and had cradled her through her withdrawals and had formed a bond with her from the beginning. Emily was not a typical foster child abused by the State, her family, and the system, she was a Macneely from birth and her future was bright Ed thought. The Macneelys decided against using him as their attorney because he was too jaded and biased in his thoughts regarding children.

Looking at the image of the adult Emily holding the package with Dave, Linda knew the Macneelys had been right from the beginning. Emily was special and beat the odds stacked against her. Linda and Ed knew they had her from the beginning and had broken the family curse of her birth parents. Emily had a clean slate to make her way in life without the baggage of her parents and the Macneelys wanted to keep her away from that shackle. It was preposterous in their minds to re-insert her into the same family that had created one of her parents, but that was the State's decision. It was almost as if they wanted to create future trouble.

Seeing how beautiful Emily was in Dave's picture made the loss of her the last couple decades even more painful for Linda. The whole system was designed to destroy lives, but Emily made it against all the odds and while no one would give the Macneelys credit for the foundation she had, Linda knew the smiling Emily in the picture overcame the odds and proved that lawyer wrong. Emily made it Linda thought, and we missed it all.

Dave texted, "Mission Accomplished, she knows." He did not call after sending the picture. Linda waited a number of minutes to see if he followed up the text and picture with a phone call. The call did not come, so she punched in her favorites where Dave was listed and heard the phone ringing on the other end. Dave answered and said, "Hello ma'am. She has the package and we talked about her first parents briefly. It went better than I ever could have imagined."

Linda started crying and could not stop. Dave just waited, listening to decades of Emily tears flowing down the face of a woman he had never even met in person, but knew better than he knew his own wife through their shared suffering. Linda cried and cried and cried, attempting to mumble something through the sobs occasionally, but nothing was intelligible. Dave could not understand what she was saying through her tears, but he dared not hang up.

Eventually the phone went dead. Linda had hung up and ended the call without ever saying anything Dave could comprehend. A few minutes later, a text came through apologizing. Linda explained she just could not speak after seeing Emily with the package from Ed and knowing it was an invitation to the funeral for the dad she did not remember, but who's entire life was altered through his two year love affair with the daughter that was stolen from him. Linda had never seen Ed with a young child and happy, before Emily or after. Being a pastor he was always around other people's children, but it was a requirement of the job and not something he wanted to do, except with Emily. Emily made Ed better than he was.

Emily changed Ed. He had driven through a snowstorm to rescue her the night she was born. Ed held her in the prison like he was her biological father. Ed then drove her home like her birth dad under normal circumstances would do. Emily was every bit Ed's daughter and Linda could see it from day one. Ed would talk to little Emily and plan a future and Emily would just eat it up. When Ed sat down, Emily came running to him. When Ed entered the room, Emily grabbed something and brought it to him. Linda was the one, who stayed up all night with her, but Emily clearly favored her daddy, and everyone knew it when they saw them together.

As the primary cook in the family, it was Ed's cooking she first consumed and loved. Ed was the reader and fun parent, while Linda was the caregiver and nurturer. Together they formed a great parenting duo and Emily flourished in their care, up until the day she was stolen. Emily may have started out behind other babies due to her drug exposure and lack of proper nutrition in the womb, but by the time the State had ruled in the aunt's favor and taken Emily, she was exceeding the averages and thriving.

Linda could not believe their long lost sweet baby was holding an invitation to her dad's funeral. Dropping to her knees, Linda began praying and thanking God for looking out and loving Emily through the tragedy of losing her first parents. Linda thanked God that Emily thrived with her aunt and uncle and that they had provided for her. Linda thanked God for the endurance that brought this day to its conclusion. Ed did not live to hold his daughter again, but she was learning the truth about her daddy now and hopefully she would come to Ed's funeral and see how much love she had received early on.

Linda could not speak on the phone, but she thanked God again for His faithfulness to her and Ed and their sweet baby, before sending Dave a text thanking him for his service and commitment. Linda promised to call him soon for a wrap up about the meeting and his sentiment regarding Emily and how she handled hearing the truth. Linda explained she just could not speak right now, so Dave would have to wait..

Chapter Five: Emily Calls Mom

Emily had decisions to make. The funeral was rapidly approaching and she had not decided to attend yet. While the plane ticket was already purchased and on her kitchen counter, she did not have a motel room and had not sought time off from work. Nothing like this is as easy as it ever seems it should be she thought, let alone for a man and family she did not know, but had claimed to know her and love her and was in desperate desire for her to attend.

Why would they want me there anyways? What could it possibly accomplish for me to attend the funeral of my "first dad," for lack of a better understanding, when I had not seen or spoken to him in decades and did not really remember him at all? These thoughts were consuming Emily's days and nights, but they would end soon, whether she went or not. Or would they? If she chose not to go, would she ever be able to rest knowing there was more to her story than she had been led to believe her whole life? Emily did not think she would be able to resist contacting her first mom and the longer and more she thought about things, she began thinking she should reach out to Linda Macneely before the funeral.

Imagine losing your husband and knowing your estranged daughter was invited, but not knowing if she would show or not. Emily was imagining the additional strain this was likely placing on the new widow and wanted to not only hear from Linda's mouth the story of their lives, but also to offer comfort and emotional aid if she could, considering the loss. Emily decided over a breakfast of sausage and eggs that she would call her first mom that evening.

The whole day drug on forever. Knowing the monumental event that was planned for the evening, the day dragged on forever and Emily could barely stand it. Every phone call, every text message, and every email seemed like it was unnecessary and such a useless distraction from the phone call to her first mom. Emily could not eat lunch, had no interest in speaking with anyone, but day dreamed and doodled all day long thinking about what her first mom would sound like and what she might say. The unknown known was absolutely terrifying, but it was also exhilarating.

As Emily pulled into her home, she realized she did not even remember getting in the car. Much like the day had been, Emily just went through the motions driving home. She backed out of her parking space, drove out of the lot and does not remember even one time looking for other cars or pedestrians. She was so distracted she could not remember looking to her left or right when she pulled into traffic and cannot believe she managed to follow the traffic rules and laws without getting in trouble. The term "distracted driver," explained her daze, because the call to Linda was blotting out the horizon. Every thing besides the phone call was dwarfed.

Emily thought she might eat first, but when it came to fixing dinner, she could not think of a single thing she wanted. A shower might calm her nerves she thought to herself, but when it came to picking out clean clothes for the night to relax in, she just could not contain the thoughts of her first mom. What was she doing? How was she handling the funeral details and loss of her husband? Were people bringing her food or was she being left alone? Did Linda have pets that were wondering where Ed was, or did they not like pets? Since Emily could not remember much, if anything about the Macneelys, these kinds of questions dominated her thoughts and would not allow her to relax.

She needed to call Linda Macneely and put these thoughts to rest, if not for Linda's sake, for her own. Emily grabbed her phone and looked at the documents from Dave Johnson with Linda's contact information. She dialed the phone number, but held off on pushing send because she felt like hyperventilating. It was a good thing she did not try eating, she might have lost her food with the tension. "It is just a phone call Emily! If you don't like it or feel weird, just hang up and block the number," she said to herself in an effort to pump up her courage and prepare herself for those first words.

How would Linda answer the phone? What was her voice like? Would it go to voice mail and if it did, what will I do, thought Emily to herself. Then, taking a deep breath and pausing two seconds, Emily pushed send and watched the screen as it went through the connecting motions. The phone dialed and began ringing as Emily was holding a lifeline that went back in time twenty-five years to a life she did not know and a past she never had, and the future she was denied. Emily could barely hold the phone to her ear she was so nervous about hearing the voice from the other end. Then she heard the connection. The phone was answered and the first words in decades were spoken between mother and daughter as Linda said, "hello?"

Emily stayed silent. It was not on purpose. Her mouth was moving but nothing was happening or coming out. She was not avoiding responding. She just couldn't. She knew the voice on the other end was Linda Macneely's. Emily knew the voice. Her mind was screaming to her and her skin was tingling as goose bumps covered her from head to tow.

Emily discovered, with the hearing of only one word from Linda, that Linda Macneely's voice was the voice in her head her whole life. All of her life when she had debates with herself about decisions and things to do, the voice in her head spoke with the same intonation, inflection, and tone as Linda Macneely. Emily could not believe the connection in her mind with Linda had never left. Her first mom's voice was the editor in her mind. Her first mom's voice was the voice of reason when she made decisions. Her first mom's voice was the sound of correction when she did wrong that made her want to make amends. Linda Macneely's voice was always known and never left her.

Linda Macneely is my mother and I know her, Emily thought. How could I have never known my inner voice was my mothers, Emily asked herself? It all seemed so strange and almost as if her whole life came full circle when she heard Linda say, "hello."

"Hello, is anyone there," asked Linda again? "I am hanging up if you do not respond."

"Mom…..," and then the tears started gushing. It was all Emily could get out. Emily's tears began flowing and running down her face and her tongue got so heavy she could not speak and could barely breathe. Her tears were so plentiful; they were like waterfalls after the spring snow melt of a long winter. Emily was coughing and snotting and could not say another word. She knew Linda Macneely!

Emily's mind was blown and her heart was rapidly beating. Linda's voice is the voice of comfort I have always known and now I know where it came from. Emily may have been taken from the Macneelys at two, but they were not erased from her mind. Her mind had held onto them and kept them alive in the background of her life. Emily's mind gave the Macneelys an important role to help her steer her way through trouble and decisions. Linda Macneely may not have been there every day in the physical sense, but her first mother had always been there through this voice in her head. Emily loved and was loved by this voice.

It was not a lot different for Linda. Linda Macneely heard, "Mom" come through her phone and stopped cold. She could not say a word because she knew it was Emily on the other end after all these years. Linda could not even breathe for fear of losing connection, even though she had been hoping this call would come through. This phone call was the only reason she answered the phone.

Looking at the phone she had immediately noticed the area code. Linda had looked at the phone number and realized it was the one number she had memorized without ever calling. It was the number she had dialed thousands of times because she would not allow herself to put Emily into her contacts.

Linda always wanted to call Emily and had dialed the number more times than she could count, but she never hit send. Emily had called her and said, "Mom!" Could this be?

"Emily, is that you?" Linda could not say another word. Her tears began running down her cheeks. In no time her shirt was soaked and her sleeves covered in wet patches as she wiped the new tears off. After all these years and the thousands of Emily tears she had shed in painful memory, these were the best tears ever. My Emily is on the phone and called me, Linda thought. Ed's death had brought them together, just like he thought it would. Two women, madly in love with each other twenty-five years ago, separated by decades and thousands of miles, who had been connected in the heart and soul, were reconnecting again.

Linda felt fear assault her in violent waves. She was deathly afraid of saying the wrong thing and driving her Emily away. A million thoughts and a million times this conversation had occurred in her mind and in her dreams as she slept and piddled around, but now it was happening in real life and what would she say? What might drive Emily away and what might keep her on the phone? Linda had no idea because she wanted to speak to Emily so bad about so many things, but could not even get the first sentence out to its conclusion. Fear gripped her heart because she was already dreading the end of the call.

Linda and Emily both heard tears and crying coming from the other end of the phone. This was a reunion of two broken hearts and two hurting souls that had been separated for a long time. Ed would be so happy to know this was happening Linda thought. "Ohhh, Ed," she said to herself as she stared at the roof of their house, "Emily called."

"Emily, I am so happy to hear from you. I cannot describe or tell you how much I have wanted to hear your voice. It has been decades since I heard your voice. You sound like I always thought you must. Your voice is so beautiful."

"Mom, I am sorry......," but Emily could not finish her sentence. The tears and the snot were choking her voice. As the word sorry escaped her lips and her voice cracked, she realized there was a life she was denied and opportunities and chances she was never going to have, because the State had chosen her aunt and uncle over the Macneelys. Emily felt stuck between a rock and a hard place because her aunt and uncle had raised her and given her everything a child could want, but they had never given her the love she was hearing in Linda's voice.

Emily could tell there was a difference. Linda Macneely had suffered for her every single day and suffered in silence with her now dead husband Ed. They had loved a child and lost. They were denied her childhood as much as she was denied her own childhood. They were all forced to live through someone else's corrupt decision. Emily's aunt and uncle had been great, but they forced Emily to live a childhood not of her own choosing. They had manipulated the system and now Emily was coming to understand, just from the handful of words she heard Linda speak, the kind of love she missed out on and why her aunt wanted to keep them apart.

Linda responded to Emily's brief apology by saying, "Emily, you have nothing to apologize for. Ed and I have to apologize to you. We did not know how wicked and evil and corrupt the DHHS people were. We had no idea they would collude with the adoption agency to sell you on the open market to your aunt for profit. We did not know. We trusted God would keep you with us forever and were blind-sided to lose you. Emily, please accept our apology and forgive us. Ed died a man of sorrow at losing you and failing to keep you protected and it has framed every day of our lives since we lost you. Can you ever forgive us?"

"Mom, how can I forgive that which I never knew? I was never told about you guys in any concrete ways. I had no idea I had a first mom and dad that loved me. I thought I had wicked Christian foster parents that were using me for money because that is what I was told. Can you ever forgive me for not knowing and not seeking you out sooner to learn the truth?"

"Emily, we love you more than life itself. We never stopped loving you and praying for you and being your parents, even if we were not there in person. If you ever get the chance and want to listen to your daddy preach I want you to pay attention. If you listen real close you will hear him mention you often. You were the biggest source of pain and loss either of us ever felt or knew, but also our biggest source of joy and love.

37

Every single day we prayed for you. We recruited thousands of churches, pastors, and Christians the whole world over to pray for you weekly. Emily, you may be the most prayed and protected person in the history of the world."

"I did not know any of this mom, but it does explain why I always felt a sense of security and safety outside of my aunt and uncle. In everything I ever did, I never felt fear or hesitation. I always felt like I had a guardian angel looking out for me my whole life. Mom, did you know the still voice in my head that I have heard my whole life is yours? You have always been with me and I never knew."

Hearing Emily say the voice in her head that spoke to her and aided her sounded like Linda's voice brought a fresh onslaught of tears to Linda. It was like God was emptying the wells again to flood the earth, the tears were so thick and numerous. Linda felt a lifetime of pain leaving her with every syllable Emily said. She felt the love for Emily she had not been able to give directly to her, was finally coming out. They did not have to say much, even if they could have, because with each new path their conversation went, fresh tears flowed on both sides of the phone.

Eventually they cleared the initial passion and could truly begin repairing the damage of their decades apart. Emily asked about her two years and Linda filled in all the gaps her aunt and uncle did not know or never told her about. She learned about the tremors she had the first six months as the drugs worked their way out of her system. How she had trouble sleeping and Linda had stayed up every night with her, often falling asleep with her on her chest. The stories Linda told Emily brought to mind all the things she had missed.

Hearing about her past began jarring dormant memories loose. Emily asked if they had a brown leather couch and two dogs when she was a baby. Linda told her they did have two dogs, although one died the week after she was stolen from them. Both of the dogs had loved her, even if they did knock her down a few times and gave her a bruise or two. Emily said she remembered the peaceful feeling of sleeping and napping on someone's chest, but did not know it was Linda's. More tears began flowing as Emily realized so much of her childhood was a lie.

Linda told Emily how much she loved Ed's cooking. Ed was the primary cook and when he was in the kitchen, little Emily would come in there and stand on his feet while he cooked, Linda explained. Almost every morning they would begin the day with either sausage and eggs or bacon and eggs. Emily informed Linda this is her favorite breakfast. Emily said, "I start every single day with sausage or bacon and eggs and it is my favorite meal. On the days I am unable to start with this breakfast, I tend to be grouchy and cranky. It is my daily fuel."

Linda and Emily laughed as they realized so many of the things they did had had a lasting impact and none of them knew it. It was clear the effort to remove the Macneely influence in her life was strong, but their love and parenting had had a strong influence from the foods Emily preferred to the voice in her head. There were so many things they talked about from their two years together that before either Linda or Emily knew it, the clock was striking three chimes in the background.

When Emily asked what happened for her to be taken, Linda said, "So much you would not believe me if I told you. That was why Ed included the court transcript in the package. He wanted to make sure you knew the truth and that we were not making these things up when we say you were stolen from us and the people involved are evil and wicked tools of Satan, sent to destroy families for a pay check."

Emily asked if her aunt and uncle were part of this conspiracy and Linda said yes, but they were not the heavy lifters. They were only the causative agents that got the ball rolling. "For the first year, it seemed everyone was in favor of us adopting you. The problem was the judge kept slow rolling the court proceedings. It took a year to sever the parental rights. If our case had been in almost any other state, we would have been awarded full custody and adoption within six months and you would have never been taken. In Michigan though, the system is designed as if it was designed to solely increase the profitability of selling children on the open market."

Linda encouraged Emily to read the transcript of the proceedings, but said she would tell Emily everything she ever wanted to know. Linda described the night her and Ed drove through a huge ice storm to pick her up. How they did not arrive at the prison until three minutes before it closed for the day. "Ed had run in to the prison to get their attention and let them know I was coming. We walked through the prison's hallways and found the hospital ward and there were all these hardened female criminals in there staring at us and clapping because they knew we were coming for you."

"The nurse showed us to you and handed us a couple of forms that we filled out and then said, 'she is all yours.' They gave us some blankets and toys to bring with you the other nurses had brought for your first day of life outside the womb. It was not uncommon for babies to be born in the prison, but it was always a treat for the nurses and inmates it seemed. You were beautiful. I loved you at first sight and Ed took a picture of me holding you. It was just like I had carried you in my own womb and we left the prison with our new bundle of joy."

Emily asked about her biological mother and how well they had known her. "We did not know her well. I had spoken to her a couple of times before you were born and we had discussed being temporary parents until she got out of prison, but she was a tough one. She had a pretty long sentence already and then she kept up her life of crime behind bars and she was not going to get out anytime soon, so we mutually decided together that our home was the best and safest place for you and when she got out, if she ever got out, we would discuss letting her have a small part in your life."

"Your biological dad however wanted nothing to do with you, I am sorry to say on one hand and thankful on the other. He had a bunch of kids with other women and you were just one more in his mind and he was never going to pay a dime to support you or celebrate a birthday or anything with you, so he did not care. His other kids, your half brothers and sisters, had all been born addicted to drugs also and were damaged in different ways from their abusive mothers too."

"Emily, your starting point was not the best. The odds were stacked against you and we knew it because we had read a lot of books about drug-addicted babies. But there was hope in our minds because we prayed for you and loved you and once you got the drugs out of your system fully, you really began making strides. You were our miracle baby and the sweetest kid a person could ever meet. Everyone loved you and because your daddy was a pastor and people person, you got to meet a lot of people. It was a time of real joy for us and we were certain we would be adopting you soon."

"We went to court every month and nothing was done. Then another month would pass and nothing was done. Finally after a year your birth parents rights were terminated and we thought we would be able to adopt you. Your daddy went to the courthouse and filed a petition to adopt. The scumbag boss at DHHS, Sally Davis, when she was notified by the court we had filed to adopt you, she had the petition removed and told us we had over stepped the line. She told us she was putting you into the system for adoption and an adoption agency would make the recommendation on who would get to adopt you. Sally Davis said we were just foster parents and there was a system in Michigan that would decide who would adopt you."

"We could not believe it. We had spent a year at that point caring for you and loving on you and making plans for your future, and now they were putting you up for adoption in the system so anyone could take you. We could not believe it. Sally Davis was a wicked and lying woman who was in cahoots with your aunt and uncle because they had threatened to sue her and DHHS. Davis was such a weak and corrupt individual that we learned later she hand-selected the most corrupt adoption agency in the state of Michigan to take your case because she wanted to make sure you went to your aunt and uncle."

"Really? How come I never heard any of this?"

"Think about it Emily, do you think your aunt and uncle would tell you this story about corruption and lies and how you were taken from us? It would not be in their interest for you to know the truth. They worked back channel deals to have you taken from us and awarded to them. It was an ugly and dark time in our home. We began realizing the powers that were aligned against us when your aunt and uncle would come into town every now and then and you would be taken from us and given to them for visits."

"Oh Emily, you would scream and cry and hold on tight to us because you did not want to go, but we were forced to give you to them. It was so painful because it was like we were being forced to give you away and you did not understand why your mommy and daddy were giving you away. You were too young, but the pain was real for all three of us. When you would come back in a couple of days, you would reach for us and cling to us, but what we did not know then, was they were trying to break you and the bond you had with us. Emily, you cannot imagine how wicked those people were. Everyone could see how much you did not want to go with your aunt and uncle, but they would write in their papers you loved it and had no issue leaving us. They are terrible and evil liars."

"Emily, you have no idea how much they circle the wagons and protect each other. Your GAL was in on the scandal the whole time. She was supposed to be your advocate, but she just went along with everything the corrupt people at DHHS and the adoption agency said. She had seen you with us and watched you flourishing, but because she was being paid by DHHS and the system, she went right along with them and the decision to have you removed and given away. She is a soulless person that earned some silver at your expense, while gaining a one way ticket to hell."

"The adoption agency people began coming to our home after your biological parents rights were severed. They would make these wild accusations and treat us like dirt before they left for the day. We did not know it at the time, but they were writing up these terrible reports about us; they said we were a threat and risk to your future. They wanted to take you and give you to your aunt and away from us and in the process the federal government would give them $10,000 if it could be done in 90 days or less."

"You won't believe this Emily. On day 89 the adoption agency submitted their recommendation that you be taken from our care immediately and given to your aunt. They earned their blood money and stole you out from under us. We had no idea it was the last time we would ever see you. We were such fools Emily! They called us and said we could spend one hour with you, heavily supervised, and then you were flying away with your aunt and we would never see you again. You daddy went to the courthouse to get an injunction, but learned they had a secret hearing without us the day prior, which was against the law, and the judge had signed off on your removal already. The things these people did to remove you were pure evil."

"How did they get away with it?"

"Emily the system is rigged. When the Bible says we should not expect justice and righteousness in this world, it is spot on. The devil controls the courts and the State and all of its functionaries. You were sacrificed on the altar of the State. Your childhood was stolen and you were sold for $10,000. We fought and had a hearing and all of their lies were exposed, but it did not matter. The weak-willed judge even said, 'I would give you Emily if it was in my power, but since they decided on the aunt I will honor it.' Even though he knew it was wrong!"

"The judge could have overturned the ruling, but he had made a career from the State and he was not going to jeopardize his retirement. We would often see these people together in the courthouse and around town. They were all friends and all earned their livelihood destroying other people's lives. These people are pawns of the devil in his fight against God and they are well compensated for their trouble in this life. Just read the transcript and you will see how the adoption agency admits they lied. You will see how the State's adoption board admits the information in the report they based their decision on were all false and untrue. You will hear the words of people vouching for how well you were doing in our care compared to the write up that said we were a hazard to your future."

"Emily, you were stolen from us plain and simple, but I do not want you to hold it against your aunt and uncle. Ed and I had hard feelings for them for many years, but we came to realize DHHS and the adoption agency and your GAL were feeding them lies about us so they would take you and they could all get paid the bonus. Your aunt and uncle, who knows what stories they were told about us, but I am sure they heard some whoppers and because of this, they wanted to save you from harm. They are not innocent, but they are also much less guilty than the State officials that did the devils dirty work for a bag of silver."

Emily could not believe all of the things she was hearing. She had read the transcript and it did not make sense to her because she did not understand the context of the Macneely appeal. Now that she heard the context and what happened, she began to understand just how deeply depraved the people that took her away from the Macneelys were. They had lied about everything regarding the Macneelys and when you read the transcript, their lies all came out, but the judge, a weak-willed individual sided with the State anyways instead of showing the balls to actually deliver justice. Now it all made sense.

Emily could see from the transcript and the words of Linda why her aunt and uncle had thought such terrible things about the Macneelys. They had also been lied to and did not know the extent of the lies against the Macneelys. Her aunt and uncle were guilty of threatening to sue if they were not given a fair shake at adopting her, but they had not lied and committed the crimes against her person the people at DHHS, the GAL, or the adoption agency had done that the judge approved. Emily felt sick about what happened to her.

Of course her aunt and uncle had done well by her, but they never loved her. Now it was making sense. They felt they had rescued their niece from terrible people and had been instrumental in the process. Her aunt and uncle thought they had saved her from a terrible upbringing because they had been fed lies by the same people that hurt the Macneelys. The system was rigged and deceived everyone to make more money off her case. She was sold like a commodity and now it was all coming out and was so clear. The love she always craved was in the Macneely home and was always there, she just did not know it.

Emily was feeling the pain of Linda and Ed come through the phone as her unknown story came out. She had sympathy for them and understood now why they had stayed away and did not want to cause her any confusion. They loved her more than life itself and denied themselves the pleasures of life on her behalf so she could thrive as best she could in the situation that was thrust upon her and them. Emily realized the parents and love she always wanted had always been there and now would always be present. There was no doubt in her mind she would come to Ed's funeral and she did not need a motel room, she would stay with Linda.

Chapter Six: Aunt Terry Again

Emily did not expect her aunt and uncle to call and say they were coming over, but they did. When Terry and Bill arrived, they quickly sat down and asked Emily to join them. Terry took the reins and Bill mostly sat quietly to the side. Terry explained to Emily that she could not go to Ed's funeral. In Terry's mind they had rescued Emily from life as a Christian and not just any Christian, but a fundamentalist Christian and Southern Baptist upbringing.

Terry and Bill both felt Emily would have grown up inside a cult where she would have been brain washed and treated as a second-class citizen because she was a female. In their minds there was nothing worse than Christians, except Christians who took it so seriously they tried to follow biblical principals. Emily asked them what they had against Christians and where they got their information and both of them explained they had gone to Catholic school as a kid and they learned all they needed to know about Christianity there.

In their minds, they had rescued Emily from the kind of life where she would never know her full potential. "Those Baptists," Terry said, "actually believe the Bible. They give money to their churches and oppose abortion! These are not normal people and they oppose almost everything we have raised you to believe in. We saved you from their crazy thinking and backward ways, Emily."

"But mom, I do not agree with your point of view. I do not think Christians are what is wrong with the world. Sin is what is wrong with the world. People are sinful and if they can be forgiven and move beyond their past, most people I have met feel they are more free than they have ever been, upon believing in Jesus."

"My God Bill, after one small contact she is already talking like one of them. Has all of our effort to raise you to be progressive like us come undone already, after one contact? Emily what has happened to you? We put a lot of time and money into you and now you are turning your back on everything we raised you to believe in?"

"I never bought what you were selling mom. I have watched you almost my entire life. You have always been the least willing person to accept others if they do not agree with you, but you call yourself a progressive and tolerant. I just want to be free. Why do I have to register to vote? Why do I have to be a Democrat to be any good in your eyes? Why do I have to rely on government to provide me anything? The government has never done anything good in the world that I can see and it ripped me from the home of my first parents."

"Emily, the government is the solution to the world created by all these fundamentalist Christians. If they and their God had their way, we would all be forced to pray and go to church. Does that sound like freedom to you?"

"Mom, that is just absurd. How many times have you ever been forced to go to church, or been forced to give money to a church, or to even pray at anytime against your will? Forcing people to convert or support someone else's beliefs is what government does, not Christianity."

Bill, so quiet and so infrequent to speak up interjected, "Emily, where did you learn to think like this? We never encouraged this kind of thinking. We never spoke like this or harbored these kinds of thoughts. Where did you learn to think like this? The things you are saying are opposed to everything we believe in and have raised you to believe. Where did you come up with this stuff because I know it was not in our home?"

Emily looked at Bill, "I have been thinking like this for awhile. I read Ayn Rand in high school and liked what she had to say about the individual and empowerment. Then I found that old politician Ron Paul and read a couple of his books and I liked what he said. However, things really turned around for me when I began reading the Bible on my own. Did you know Israel existed without a government and when they demanded a king, God said they were rejecting Him, just like the surrounding cultures?"

Cutting her off in mid-discussion, Terry said, "Emily, you cannot go to Ed's funeral. I forbid you from going."

"Mom, I had not fully decided whether I was going to go or not, but after listening to you guys, I think I am. I want to see and meet the Macneelys and see for myself if they are anything like you have said they are. I want to see for myself if they are the people you are saying they are or just what I missed out on."

"Emily, they are everything we have said and more. We saved you from them. You were this close to being a Baptist," as Terry held up her fingers with a small gap between them.

"I do not know why you hate them the way you do or how everything happened or what the truth is, but I want to meet these people that raised me in my early years and wanted to adopt me. I not only want to satisfy this for myself, but I owe them this kind of closure also. They wanted me, they loved me, they lost me, and now I am going to go and close the gap for them."

Terry and Bill stood up, stared at Emily, and stormed out of the house. They sped off; laying the most rubber their electric car could leave when the hammer was dropped. On the way home they talked about where they messed up and how this could be happen. Bill said, "Terry, you knew she was fine with them. You knew they loved her and had done a lot with her and that she was a wonderful baby in their care. Terry, you knew Emily was in good hands in their care when you threatened to sue if they did not give Emily to us."

"You cannot fault Emily for wanting to learn her past and just who the Macneelys are. I for one have never felt right about taking Emily from them. While it was all semi-legal, we used the law to kidnap a child and threaten a family. Honestly, I am surprised this has not happened sooner. I could tell they were never going to let her go when we took her. We should be thankful it has taken this long and that Ed is dead. You do realize Emily has never once called me, daddy. But you and I both know she was calling Ed daddy before we took her."

"Terry, we intervened in her life and changed the dynamics and family she left forever. Not only did we change her life and theirs, we have never given her the kind of love they would have given her. If you cannot see that even now and how wrong we were to take her, then you are blind. I understand you hate Christians, but we stole their kid and destroyed a family. Let her go and hope she comes home. She might never want to see us again, especially after today."

Chapter Seven: The Funeral

Linda and Emily rode to the funeral together. They were going to hire a car to drive them, but the brother Emily never had a chance to meet said he would bring them early to the church. Billy Macneely was already a college graduate and married by the time the Macneelys tried to adopt Emily. He never even had a chance to meet her in person when she was an infant because he had been living in a different state working on his seminary degree. Billy may not have met Emily in person, but having been raised by the Macneelys, he knew what kind of attention she received as a baby from his mom and dad.

As parents they could not be any more different, but together they provided the exact kind of home a kid needed. Linda, his mom, was over bearing and protective, constantly trying to protect and shelter and keep her children safe from harm. His mom believed in washing ones hands and wearing clean clothes and avoiding sick people. She was a real mother hen, which was totally opposite of his dad.

Ed was a rough and tumble no shenanigans kind of guy. Ed always encouraged him to take the risk and push the envelope. Ed was the pusher while Linda was the anchor. Because of their differences in parenting, most people found Ed grumpy and unpleasant, but to any who knew him they knew this was not true. Ed was always working hard to open the whole world and expand the horizons for his children and Billy knew Emily was being raised in a great home with loving parents. Billy always regretted how his time back then never allowed for him to bring his new wife to visit his parents when they had Emily.

Billy had picked Emily up at the airport. The hug he laid on her caught her by surprise. She could not believe this strange older man considered himself her brother, even though they never met and she had not been a part of the family for the last two and half decades. Billy explained that just because she had not been there, a person could not spend much time with either of his parents the last twenty-five years and not hear all about Emily. They were so proud of her that they could not help but speak about her to everyone, including him,

Emily asked, "Do you ever get jealous?"

"No, I never have. I never doubted my parents loved me and they made sure I knew, but you were taken from them so it was acute. You have no idea how many plans they had made before you were taken. Unfortunately, man often makes plans and life intervenes and changes course."

"So even though you never met me, you still consider me your sister?"

"Emily, just because you were not present, does not mean you were not there. Every single holiday, you were there and we prayed for you. Every single birthday, yours and ours, you were there and prayed for and missed. Every single milestone in any of our lives, we celebrated as if you were there and present. We have never lived like you were not here, even though we never knew if you would be again. My parents have lived their life since you were taken as if you were still there. Have you not listened to any of the old man's sermons?"

"No, I have not listened to any yet, but I should so I can hear his voice and messages. Was he a real Bible-thumper?"

"You are aware we are Southern Baptists right? The term Bible-thumper was invented for us. My parents try and share the Good News of Jesus on a weekly basis with people they have never met or they are getting to know. Emily, you owe it to yourself to go back to the beginning and listen going forward.

You will hear a man preaching a Biblical message with a broken heart every single week. There are so many messages he could not even get through because he missed you so bad. It is like you are in the church every time he gets behind the pulpit and he has left a lifetime tribute to you in his sermons. You really should listen."

Emily and Billy stopped for some pizza on the way back to the house, bringing dinner home for the family. Emily had asked for people not to barrage her as this was not her day, it was Ed's and Linda needed the peace and quiet of putting his memory to rest. The four of them, with Billy's wife Dawn, ate the pizza and stayed up all night talking about Ed and his life. Emily learned things about her first dad she did not know and was gracious and thankful to hear. He was clearly a man of integrity that loved her more than she knew a man could love.

Her feelings towards Ed were novel because she did not know men or dads could love the way Ed did. Her aunt and uncle had not modeled the same kind of lives as the Macneelys. The more time she spent in the presence of the Macneelys, the more she realized how much the State had robbed her of joy. She had never experienced joy in her life and was always sad and never knew why, but now she did. Subconsciously she knew there was more to life and she was robbed of a childhood and love. It was not that her aunt and uncle were bad people and parents, they just were not loving people and she always felt like they would have been more happy if her mother had aborted her.

Emily could never figure out why they wanted her throughout her life. Now though she was beginning to understand why they sought her out. They had been fed lies that the Macneelys were bad people and Christian, although there was not a distinction between bad and Christian in their worldview, so they felt obligated to rescue her. Her whole childhood was beginning to make sense now. They did not want her, but felt obligated to rescue her and this impacted everything about their parenting towards her.

In her own mind, Emily was beginning to see how the Macneelys truly suffered for her benefit and how much they had given up when the State had taken her. By this point, she had a pretty good idea about who her first parents were. She did not know what to expect with the funeral, the church building was not overly large where Ed was pastor, so she did not expect many more than the people in the family she already met and the members of the church.

Billy and Dawn had gone outside thirty minutes prior, which put them ready on time. They encouraged Emily to join them and said their mother was always late and as dad always said, she would be late even to his funeral. Emily said she would stick around and help her mom, but after trying to get Linda moving quicker for fifteen minutes, Emily said she was going outside with Billy and Dawn. The three of them sat in the vehicle laughing about late people and waiting on Linda, who truly was going to be late to her own husbands funeral.

Pastor Ron, the associate pastor was scheduled to conduct the service and had been encouraging people to take their seats and get ready by the time the Macneelys arrived for Ed's funeral. The time for greeting and sharing was skipped because Linda was late and brought the kids with her, late as always. Pastor Ron knew Linda, as did everyone else, so no one was surprised she was late to the funeral. Linda always tried her best, but she just could not be on time. Ed had fought this battle on a daily basis with Linda and even by the time of his death, was still losing every single time.

Linda slowly walked to the front and sat down. She was wearing black, looked extremely beautiful and young for an older lady in her 60's, and clearly was barely holding things together. Ed had tried to explain the funeral plans to her over the years, but she had never really listened, she just knew Ed had planned his own funeral for many years and had centered the whole thing on Emily. Linda was not jealous Ed focused his own funeral on his lost daughter and not his wife or son, she knew the pain he had experienced and how the loss impacted him over the years.

What she did not know was what the plan was or how the funeral would be conducted. She was wishing she would have paid attention over the years, but here she was, finding out for the first time. Pastor Ron asked everyone to take a seat. He asked everyone to turn to their program and review the timeline and schedule of events.

The whole church began laughing as they looked at the program as it said, 11:00 scheduled time for the service to begin. 11:45, Linda shows up late and everyone can be seated. It appears Ed banked on Linda being late and planned for it in the schedule and everyone was laughing about it. Point goes to Ed, which is exactly what he put inside parenthesis next to the 11:45 AM, time for Linda's arrival. Ed always had a sense of humor and he knew his wife well. What he did not know, but had hoped for, was that his whole family would be united again.

The planned funeral called for two songs, both of which were favorites of Ed's. The church began singing, "Why Me," by Kris Kristofferson and remembered how many times as a group they had sung this song together as the tears flowed. The nut shell of the song being, "Why me, Lord?" What did I ever do to receive this reward and blessing after a life of sin and destruction? Ed loved this song, because it showed the great mercy of Jesus and God's ultimate plan of redemption and forgiveness for all who believe and profess faith in Jesus.

After singing the second song, Pastor Ron said he had two videos and was instructed to play one or the other depending on who was in attendance. As the church began looking around, all eyes rested on Emily as Ron said, "With Emily being here, I have a special video from her dad that I recorded with him a number of years ago. Ed wanted to make sure his words were captured because he never expected to live into his late 60's." Hitting play on the video, the lights were dimmed, and people saw a giant image of the deceased fill the screen.

Ed stared at the screen for a second before he began speaking. For the audience, they could not tell if he was waiting for the record button to get pushed or if he was gathering himself and his composure. Then Ed began speaking to the camera and all doubt was erased. "My sweet Emily. You have always been my sweet baby. I love you. To my family and friends, I apologize for never really being there as much as I should have been. I was always with Emily in my mind. There has not been a moment every day I am not praying and pleading her case to God."

"I know this sounds bad, but when I was at your house, eating your chow, and sharing an enjoyable time with you, I was only partly there because I was thinking about my sweet baby and who was looking out for her. When I was watching your ball games or sharing some testimony with you or even on Sundays when I was preaching, my mind and heart were always with Emily and I could not shake her. Remember all the times I got choked up and could barely speak, those were Emily's tears."

"Therefore I want to apologize to all of you, especially my wife and Billy. I owed you both my full attention, especially you Linda because you were experiencing the same trauma as me, but I could not drop Emily from my mind or my prayers. I prayed for her constantly and was always interceding on her behalf before the throne of God and it has impacted everything I have done since she was taken from us. Since this video is being played today at my funeral, I know she is here and one of my prayers has been answered. My sweet baby is back with her mother again and getting to meet her brother."

"I have no doubt she is learning the truth of her childhood and who her family is. I have no doubt Linda is showering love upon her and Billy and Dawn are enjoying the sister they always knew they had, but never met. As a church body I thank you all for coming, all of you have listened to me plead my case before God on Emily's behalf for years. You have suffered through countless sermons and prayers where my voice broke and cracked because I was thinking about Emily. I thank all of you for standing by me as I mourned and interceded on behalf of my daughter. I know you all would have done the same for your children if they had been lost in the same way, but I do not know if I would have been as compassionate as you have been towards me."

"I ask all of you to be patient with Emily and understand none of this was her fault. I have no doubt she is the sweet adult she was as a child and many of you knew. What Emily does not know is many of you were in this church and watched her grow up for two years before she was taken. Emily has been woven through the fabric of my life and through the DNA of this church and today, I present my grown daughter to you."

55

"Our prayers have been answered and she has come home and I would ask each of you to never forget her in prayers. If any doubt exists in any of you whether God exists, let the presence of Emily here today put your doubts to rest. You and I prayed for her every single day, for however long it takes for this to play. God has answered and brought her home and I ask all of you to love on her and give my wife, Billy, and Dawn some extra care, because the family is made whole in my death. Ron, you can take the pulpit again, thank you. Emily and all the rest of you, I love you."

Ron gave a small message and appealed to the crowd to love Jesus and give their lives and trust to Him who saves and not their own will. Ron urged those who wanted to attend the graveside service to allow the family access to the gravesite without having to climb over people. The local police had volunteered their time to close the intersections from the facility to the cemetery for all those who wanted to follow the hearse. As Ron came off the pew, a large body of people, some of which were church members and others who had been touched by Ed's pastoring and life stood up, turned around, and began marching to their cars because they knew Ed was not going to be late to his own internment.

At the gravesite, a large body of people surrounded the casket in open rings, showering the family with support. Ron gave another small message, only this time asking who was there and how long those in attendance had known Ed. There was a large contingent from Ed's high school days. Classmates and teammates in sports that Ed had maintained ties with over the years since they completed school together. Similarly, there was a large contingent of people from his days in the military, only some of which knew the family, as Ed had been single the first half of his time in the army.

The rest of the people were from the local body of believers and others who had read his books and gotten to know Ed from his many adventures around the area. Ed was a well-known and good man and many people had come to see his funeral, but everyone knew they were not there to see Ed off into the eternal, but to see if Emily, his long lost daughter would show up and give him peace. Ron made sure Emily had a prominent position and encouraged everyone that was coming to the wake to make sure they stopped by and talked to the different members of the family. Ron closed with an invitation to follow Jesus and three hands were raised, professing a new found belief in Jesus. Ed would have been so happy to know some of his friends would be joining him in eternity because of Jesus and his presence on this day.

Chapter Eight: "Your Daddy..."

The wake was enough to make Emily's head spin. It seemed every person at the funeral wanted to speak to her. Emily was feeling guilty because people were focusing on her and almost ignoring Linda. Emily sat next to Linda and apologized for all the attention she was drawing when it should have been a day of mourning and consolation for her. Linda looked at Emily and said this is not a day of mourning, "these people loved your daddy and knew how important you were to him and they also know he is in a better place because of Jesus, so no one is sad. They just want to see and talk to you because they know how important you have been to us all these years and there is not a person here who we have not recruited to pray for you since you were stolen."

"All of these people have been praying for me? Why, would they pray for?"

"Oh Emily, you have not figured this out yet. We began praying for you before you were even born. Then when we had you we prayed over you every single day and night. It was a family time of prayer. We prayed for your health and healing and future and the husband you would have and just everything you could imagine. We pled your case before the throne of God in an effort to draw God's favor in your life and to help you. Then before they took you, we spent a lot of time praying you would not be taken and we would be able to adopt you."

"Wow. But after I was taken and given to my aunt and uncle, why did you keep praying and recruit all of these people? It seems like it was a waste of time after God did not keep me with you in the first place and let me be taken."

"Emily, I would be lying if I said we did not have the same thoughts many times. You cannot imagine how shaken we were when you were taken. We had poured so many prayers over you and so much love into you that we never figured God would allow them to take you. We were devastated when you were taken. I cannot even describe it accurately so you would understand or believe it."

As Emily and Linda spoke, the surrounding people seemed to fade into the background, even though they were surrounded by people. If there is one thing Baptists do well, it is bring food and eat when there is a reason and even when there isn't. Emily and Linda kept talking and people were lining up with plates of food and a desire to speak with Emily without interrupting Linda and Emily as they spoke. Everyone knew how important it was that these two spend time together and cover the years they have spent apart.

During a pause in their conversation, a large man with an obvious military background and demeanor, grabbed Emily's hand and said he never had a chance to meet her when she was a baby, but he knew all about her because of his friendship with Ed. "Emily, I was a soldier under your daddy. We spent a couple of years together training and deploying all over the United States and your daddy helped me get a few jobs. When I needed a reference, your daddy was my go to guy and he never failed me. I owe him a lot from the years of support and I just want you to know, your daddy was a loyal dude who never quit on any of his friends or soldiers. Even after we parted ways. I want to tell you one thing though, he never beat me in a foot race."

Once the former soldier walked off, it was like an opening in the Red Sea and people began coming up and Emily and Linda could not speak privately anymore. The people would congratulate Linda, some even hugging her, and then they would hone in on Emily. At no point in her life had she ever been the center of attention like she was today. There were church members, soldiers, friends, people who had been coached by Ed, and everyone in between over the span of many decades. Clearly Ed was not the man her Aunt and Uncle led her to believe.

In fact, from what Emily kept hearing, Ed seemed like he was one heck of a man and nothing like her aunt and uncle described. Emily could not help but wonder just how and why her aunt and uncle held such negative views of the Macneelys, who obviously loved her deeply and wanted to adopt and raise her as their own. Emily could not help but realize, had the Macneelys adopted her, she would have finally had the same last name as her parents. It always bothered her that her last name was different than her aunt and uncle and it created a wedge and source of division between them because Emily never quite felt included in the family, no matter how much they said she was part of the family.

If she was part of the family, Emily thought, why wouldn't they give me their last name? Linda mentioned at one point they had planned on changing her name when they adopted her, but when the process kept getting drawn out, they changed their mind and decided they could not change her first name, but they would change her middle and last. They were going to call her Emily Ruth Macneely. Hearing this, Emily could not help breaking into tears because it was one of the things she always wanted, which was simply to be wanted and included in a family. She wanted a name.

Multiple players her daddy coached said they just knew she would have been an All American in basketball and fast pitch had she been coached by her daddy. They all said he had spoken about his plans to introduce the sports to her and keep her interested in them. They all looked forward to watching her grow up and experience great success and winning on the field of play. To a man they were disappointed and surprised she did not play any sports in school. Emily said she was a cheerleader, but her family did not like sports, so they never pushed her to get involved.

Emily realized this was an area of her life she never got to realize because the Macneelys were not allowed to finish the job they started in the way they wanted to. Emily saw the pictures on their walls and the trophies in their house of the success their own son and other adopted children experienced. Many of their adopted kids had been highly successful both on the field and in the classroom. Emily felt she would have had much the same experience, but she was never allowed to play.

As the crowd began thinning and people went home, Emily and Linda made a promise they would stay up speaking about whatever needed to be discussed, because Emily was scheduled to return home in two days. Emily had no idea how great an impact the funeral would have and how much she learned about her own life. She saw pictures on the walls she never knew existed her in different backgrounds in a professional studio. Emily was finally seeing baby pictures! They did look like a real family and she looked every bit like she was their kid. In all the family photos with her aunt and uncle, Emily always stuck out because she did not share any characteristics with them.

Emily always thought it was odd looking to be thin, attractive, and in shape while standing next to her much larger aunt and weak, sick-looking uncle in the family photos. Besides the different names, Emily clearly was not a biological daughter, but if she had been raised with the Macneelys, it looked like she would have fit right in. So many things Emily was seeing that she was robbed of had impacted their lives. Emily was thinking she would investigate whether she had any potential recourse with a lawsuit against the State and the adoption agency over the life she did not have through their corruption and wickedness.

Chapter Nine: Parting Again

Emily and Linda woke up on the day of Emily's flight home and had a bountiful breakfast. Emily reminded Linda her favorite breakfast was sausage, eggs, and toast. Linda said, "I already knew that. The first time you had it, you were sitting in the living room while Ed was cooking and you kept walking in on him and he kept shooing you out because he did not want any grease to burn you. After about a half hour he brought you your very own bowl of eggs and sausage and he sat down on the floor with you."

"Both of you sat there chowing down on those sausage and eggs and you should have seen yourself. You were blown away with the taste and flavors. It was like you were falling in love. You would grab some out of the bowl in your little fist, walk over to your daddy, and put it right in your mouth, like you knew he fixed it for you special, and maybe you knew you did. That was his breakfast of choice every single day until he died. He would mix in some bacon or make an omelet sometimes instead of eggs, but his favorites were the traditional lumberjack hard working blue-collar type breakfasts. I guess he picked it up from his dad who was a Marine and carpenter."

Emily's eyes filled with tears as she reflected on the thousands of breakfasts she had eaten since she was born and how she always asked for sausage and eggs and never knew the source was her real daddy, but her mind never forgot. "You picked breakfast up from your daddy. He was a Green Beret, writer, and preacher. He picked it up from his daddy and I sure hope the legacy does not end with you. Emily, I truly hope your children will grow up eating this too and it will be one more Macneely legacy that no one, not DHHS and not adoption agencies, and not anyone else can ever take from you."

Emily said, "I promise my kids will grow up knowing this meal and I hope loving it and I will make sure they know why it is my favorite and how it has been passed down over the generations to them." Emily looked at Linda and the thoughts in her mind returned again, "Oh how I love this woman. While I do not really remember much, she feels so good and so comfortable and I know for a fact there is love between us."

Looking at the "I Love Lucy" clock on the wall, Linda said we better start heading towards the airport if you are going to make your flight. Ed would never forgive me if I made you late for your flight. Emily, I am so glad this parting will not be like our last when they stole you from us. I have cried thousands of times at the way they ripped you from our arms and our home, but I am glad to see how well you have turned out. You owe your aunt and uncle a thank you when you get home."

"No mom, I owe God a thank you for bringing me to you first, so you could cover me in prayer all these years. My whole life makes sense now, where it never did before. Sure, I missed out on the child hood you guys would have given me, but I met people who exposed me to God and I always felt loved and protected, even if it was not from my aunt and my uncle. You are right, they did provide shelter and food and everything I required, but they never provided me with the love I needed and they robbed me from my real mom and dad."

Linda and Emily hugged, shedding tears in the process and messing up both of their make up jobs, before releasing each other and grabbing the luggage and heading to the car. When they backed out of the driveway, Emily noticed a giant picture the neighbors had erected of her as a baby in Ed's arm and placed on their lawn. Underneath the picture it said, "Daddy's girl and daddy have both come home."

There was not a lot of talk on the way to the airport. The thickness of the emotion and the pending departure loomed so large, neither Emily nor Linda wanted or could speak. Linda tried to tell Emily how much it meant that she had come and how important it was to her daddy that she learn something about her first couple of years and the family she was taken from, but the words did not come out easy.

Emily asked Linda if she could ask something very big. Linda said of course and Emily said, "Mom, would you adopt me now? I want to be a Macneely. Actually, I understand I have always been a Macneely, I just want to make my name line up with reality for once. I think this will give me one of those things I never had. The sense of family and fitting in and of course buckets and buckets of endless love."

Linda looked at Emily and without even hesitating, said, "Yes. Ed would love that. I will call our attorney when I get home and get everything ready and send whatever I need together to send to you so we can make this official. Oh Emily, this is the sweetest thing I have every heard of and more than I could have ever expected, but Ed always knew you would be back."

Emily, looking at Linda behind the wheel said, "I have one more thing. I have always had this small Seahawks pennant. It was on my wall my whole life and my aunt finally admitted before coming here it was the only thing they kept of my early possessions because they were also Seahawk fans. I have had this one small piece of you guys my whole life and now I have the whole package. Can I give this back to you and maybe you can hang it on the wall in the living room or somewhere and think of me every time you see it?"

"Oh Emily. I remember that pennant, I remember your daddy giving it to the adoption worker and asking that it go with you. Do you know how many times he asked me, "Do you think Emily still has that pennant? Do you think she is a Seahawks fan? Do you think she knows where it came from if she does?" Your daddy thought about you all the time Emily. I know for a fact he thought about you more than he ever thought about anything else in life. You were his girl."

As Emily and Linda parted at the airport, Emily tears flowed from both of them and they knew they would never be far apart again, no matter how far they were from each other. Linda was going to sell the house and be a free agent and figure something out, whatever it was. By the time Emily landed back home, she had decided she wanted to move and live with her mom. As soon as her baggage came off the carousel and she made it to her vehicle. She called up Linda.

"Mom, I know I already asked you one big thing in being adopted, but I would like to ask you something else now too."

"Of course Emily. I have been missing you since you left. I am so happy to hear your voice again. We must not be strangers ever again."

"Well mom, that is kind of it. I was wondering what you thought about this. Would you mind if I moved home and lived with you? You could still sell your house if you wanted and we could move wherever you wanted to go or we could stay there, it does not matter to me. I can and will work anywhere, but I do not have a mother anywhere so I want to live with you and try and get back some of what we lost the last 25 years."

Through her Emily tears, Linda said, "Yes, I would love that. Come as quick as you can with as much as you want or leave everything behind. Just come as quick as you can, we will figure it out together, mom and daughter."

ABOUT THE AUTHOR

Ian Minielly is a one time infantryman and Green Beret. He studied Psychology at Washington State and went to seminary at Liberty University Baptist Theological Seminary. Minielly spent another eight years as an intelligence analyst before becoming a pastor and author.

Many days Minielly wakes up after dreaming about jumping out of airplanes, walking long miles, shooting rifles, and riding shotgun. The dreams are usually good, but the aches and pains in his hips, knees, ankles, and back always remind him the infantry is a young man's game.

Made in the USA
Middletown, DE
06 October 2021

49736633R00045